NICK JR. The BACKYARDIGANS™

Backyardigans and the Beanstalk

by Catherine Lukas

illustrated by Susan Hall

SIMON SPOTLIGHT/NICK JR.

New York   London   Toronto   Sydney

Based on the TV series *Nick Jr. The Backyardigans*™ as seen on Nick Jr.®

SIMON SPOTLIGHT
An imprint of Simon & Schuster Children's Publishing Division
1230 Avenue of the Americas, New York, New York 10020
© 2008 Viacom International Inc. All rights reserved. NICK JR., *Nick Jr. The Backyardigans*,
and all related titles, logos, and characters are trademarks of Viacom International Inc.
NELVANA™ Nelvana Limited. CORUS™ Corus Entertainment Inc.
Manufactured in the United States of America
10 9 8 7 6 5 4 3
ISBN-13: 978-1-4169-4779-0
ISBN-10: 1-4169-4779-5

It was a beautiful spring day. Tyrone and Pablo were planting a garden.

"Do you have the beans, Gardener Tyrone?" asked Gardener Pablo.

"Right here!" Tyrone replied. "And I have my Super-Grow fertilizer."

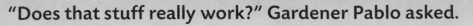

"Does that stuff really work?" Gardener Pablo asked.

"I don't know. I've never used it before," answered Gardener Tyrone as he finished sprinkling his fertilizer. Gardeners Uniqua and Austin came over to watch.

Suddenly a beanstalk zoomed out of the ground. As it grew, the stalk thickened and sprouted leaves, beans, and curling vines. Soon it reached the clouds, high over the gardeners' heads.

"Wow," said Gardener Tyrone, staring at his watering can. "This stuff works better than I thought."

"Come on!" said Gardener Uniqua. "Let's climb the beanstalk and see where it leads!"

Up, up, up they climbed. As they reached the clouds, the beanstalk became narrower and narrower. It began to bend and sway.

"Help!" yelled Gardener Pablo as he lost his footing.

Gardener Tyrone climbed to the top first. He lay down and leaned over, reaching out.

"Grab hold of my hand!" said Gardener Tyrone. He heaved his friends to safety one by one.

"It looks like we're in someone's garden," Gardener Uniqua said, looking around. "A big, royal garden!"

An enormous castle loomed in front of them.

"I wonder who lives there," mused Gardener Uniqua.

"I hope it's not a . . .," began Gardener Pablo, but he was interrupted by thunderous footsteps. Someone was approaching!

"Fee-fie-fo-fers!" they heard. "I smell the smell of some gardeners."

Just as Gardener Pablo was whispering "Hide!" to the others, some giant black rocks bounced along the ground, causing the gardeners to slip and slide.

"Watch out for those black rocks!" Gardener Tyrone hissed.

"Those aren't rocks!" Gardener Uniqua said, her eyes wide. "It's giant pepper! Run!"

The four friends ran as fast as they could. But the giant pepper smelled so strong that the friends had to stop and sneeze.

"Achoo!" Gardeners Austin and Tyrone blew themselves to the ground. The gardeners blinked up at a giant who stood looking down at them.

"Are you g-g-g-going to eat us?" asked Gardener Pablo.

"Oh, for goodness' sake!" the giant scoffed. "Don't be ridiculous. I just need more pepper to make this bowl of mush taste better. I sure am sick of eating mush though."

"Maybe you should try growing some fresh vegetables," suggested Gardener Uniqua. "They taste a lot better than mush."

The giant looked intrigued. "Show me how to grow them," she demanded.

"The least she could do is say please," muttered Gardener Pablo to Gardener Tyrone.

They showed the giant how to plant a vegetable garden. They dug, planted, watered, weeded, and used the magic Super-Grow fertilizer. The plants grew quickly.

The giant watched them. "Gardening looks like hard work," she said with a loud yawn. Then her eyelids fluttered and she began to snore.

"She made us do all the work," grumbled Gardener Austin in a low whisper.

"And she never even said please or thank you," added Gardener Tyrone.

"Let's get out of here!" said Gardener Pablo.

"But how? We can't reach the latch of the gate," Gardener Uniqua pointed out.

"I have an idea that might work," whispered Gardener Tyrone. He walked over to a giant tomato plant and gestured to Gardener Austin to climb onto it. Then he pulled the plant back and let go.

Gardener Austin sailed over the fence and landed safely on the other side.

Next went Gardener Pablo and then Gardener Uniqua. The three friends stood on the other side of the fence, staring through the slats at Gardener Tyrone, who remained on the inside.

"Wait. How are you going to get out of there?" asked Gardener Pablo.

Luckily, Gardener Tyrone had another idea. With all of his strength, he pulled a long carrot out of the giant's garden.

With a running start, he planted one end of the carrot in the ground and then pole-vaulted over the fence, landing—*splat!*—on several tomatoes. "Yuck," said Gardener Tyrone, brushing mushy tomato off his clothes.

The giant heard the noise. Her eyelids fluttered open.

"Run for it!" yelled Gardener Uniqua.

They reached the beanstalk and quickly climbed all the way back to the ground.

But then they heard the giant tromping after them.

"She's coming! She's coming! What do we do? What do we do?" said Gardener Pablo nervously, squeezing his eyes closed.

"Calm down!" said a voice over his head.

Pablo opened one eye and looked up. It was the giant.

"I was only coming to say sorry," said the giant. "I never said thank you for planting the garden for me. And the fresh vegetables are much better than mush."

"Well, you're welcome," said Gardener Uniqua with a smile.
"Happy to garden for you. That's what gardeners do, you know."
Suddenly someone's stomach rumbled.
"All this gardening made me hungry!" said Tyrone.
Giant Tasha smiled. "Then you know what it's time for?"

"A GIANT snack," the gardeners cheered.